JESUS THE OUTL

<u>Author</u>: Sam August
<u>Publisher</u>: the s
First edition: November 05, 2024

JESUS THE OUTLAW MAGICIAN

Author: Sam August

Publisher: the same as above

First printing: November 05, 2024

Copyright ©2024 by Sam August

All rights reserved. No part of this book may be reproduced in any form without written permission from the author, except for the use of quotations in a book review.

Author's e-mail: samaugust617@gmail.com

CONTENTS

04 - PREFACE
05 - DEDICATIONS
06 - ABOUT THE AUTHORS
07 - WORDS OF THE AUTHORS
09 - IF THE WILDERNESS COULD SPEAK
10 - BRED BY THE SAME TREE
11 - THE WILL TO KILL
12 - INCONVENIENT COMMENTS
13 - GOD AND THE COW
14 - HE WILL NEVER COME BACK
15 - A LOGICAL CONCLUSION
16 - FOLLOWING JESUS' EXAMPLE
17 - SMARTER THAN JESUS
21 - CAUGHT RED-HANDED
22 - THE BAD GOOD FRIDAY
23 - GOD VS. THE BIG BANG
24 - MOTHER NATURE'S CODE NAME
25 - JESUS AND KARL MARX
26 - JESUS IN HIS OWN WORDS (cont.)
45 - THE NAKED TRUTH
46 - CRUCIFIED UPSIDE DOWN
48 - THE GREATEST MAGICIAN OF ALL TIME
52 - A DEADLY COMMERCIAL COMPETITION
55 - WHAT DIFFERENCE DOES IT MAKE?
56 - HOLY SMOKE
57 - DEAD BEFORE STEPPING OUT
58 - EARTH VS. THE HUMAN VIRUS
64 - EVIL IS COLOR-BLIND
65 - SHAME ON YOU, GOD!
66 - HERE AND IN THE BEYOND TOO
67 - BEFORE GOING TO HELL
68 - MORBID CRUELTY
69 - STUCK IN THE SHIT
70 - GOD AND THE COW (cont.)
71 - HE WILL NEVER COME BACK (cont.)

FROM BEYOND THE GRAVE

(COMMENTS FROM ANONYMOUS SPIRITS)
73 - AT LEAST I DIED WITH MY EAR ON (by X)
   74 - BLOODY WEED (by Y)
   75 - JOHN DOE
   76 - JANE DOE
   77 - HIS HOLINESS THINGAMASHIT
   78 - MR. SO-AND-SO
   79 - MISS WHATSERNAME
   80 - NOBODY
   81 - MRS. THINGUMMY
   82 - LORD THINGAMAFUCK
   83 - SOMEONE OR OTHER
   84 - MR. WHOEVER

SOME POEMS

86 - NOW IS THE ONLY THING REAL
   87 - NEVER GIVE UP THE FIGHT
   88 - OUTTA CONTROL
   89 - GOD AIN'T ON YOUR SIDE
   90 - THE SAME OLD SHIT ALL OVER AGAIN
   91 - DISCLAIMER

PREFACE

In this book you will find some stuff written by me and Jesus, whom I channeled to make our literary partnership possible. Furthermore, during the writing process, I channeled some dead people through automatic writing as well. Besides, in this book Jesus reveals that his story wasn't as dull as they say. After reading his account, you'll see it was actually a story full of adventure, magic, and bravery. Then, you'll see that, in fact, it's not an overexaggeration to say he was almost kinda like a modern-day movie hero.

Now, you see, I deem it important to highlight that contrary to popular belief, the supernatural world has nothing to do with God, for God is unreal – he is nothing more than just a figment of one's imagination.

PS: At the end of this book, you'll also find some poems written by me.

*<u>Channel</u>: to serve as a medium to enable the communication between the
   living and the dead.

*<u>Channel through automatic writing</u>: to write down what is dictated by
   a spirit.

DEDICATIONS

TO MOTHER MARY WITH LOVE

Thanks, mother Mary, for having been such a brave soul and not to have given up on me. If I was you I'da given up since long ago and thrown me in the hands of destiny. If you had done so, things surely wouldn't have ended well and I'd already be burning in hell.

<u>SAM AUGUST</u>

*Both Jesus's mother and mine had the same name. In fact, my mother was named after Jesus', of course.

———————

We dedicate this book to the gay and fearless daylight
    Which to date chases away the darkness of the night

ABOUT THE AUTHORS:
SAM AUGUST

White man of average height dropped somewhere on Earth in the second half of the twentieth century.

JESUS

Roman Jew born in Egypt on an unknown date and crucified upside down when he was about 33.

WORDS OF THE AUTHORS
A FULL-FLEDGED ATHEIST

(by SAM AUGUST)

You see, since I was little boy, I didn't feel well at the worship services my father took me to attend, but I didn't understand exactly why. Well, what I knew for real was that I hated those boring sermons, prayers and hymns of praise.

You know, he had all my siblings baptized in the evangelical church he attended, except for me, cos ev'ry time they tried to baptize me I managed to run away, though I didn't comprehend the rationale behind it...

So, life went on and when I turned 16, I rebelled against it all and stopped going to church with my father. He got pissed off, but even muttering furiously he kinda accepted it – against his will of course – and from then on our relationship turned rather sour...

Then, I stayed on the fence for most of my life, that is, in fact I believed in God without really believing in him; for deep down inside I thought it was ridiculous, illogic and fucking implausible... so, the years rolled by and only many years later I got off the fence and became a full-fledged atheist.

JESUS IN HIS OWN WORDS

"I've decided to write this book with my friend Sam for three reasons: the first one was to have fun, after all ev'ryone needs a break cos life ain't no piece of cake…" *(laughs)* (continued on page 26)

IF THE WILDERNESS COULD SPEAK

"How the hell can Christians be so sure I wasn't gay, but rather straight? But what if I was gay, mate? Would I be a victim of your hate? Anyway, just suppose I really had a lover and that he was the devil who is said to have tempted me in the wilderness – just for this fact would you love me less? Or wouldn't you pay any mind? Cos, after all, love is blind." *(laughs)*
   *by JESUS

BRED BY THE SAME TREE

"Ev'ry good tree bears only good fruit, but only bad fruit are brought forth by a bad tree. So, it's the same with politicians in man's society – they're the rotten fruit bred by the bad tree of evil and promiscuity. However, they are just the reflection of you, stupid brood of vipers who keep on swallowing the lies they tell. And as you wish you were in their shoes, I conclude you're rotten fruits as well."

*by JESUS

THE WILL TO KILL

"I once spoke this way and not like they say: "If someone slaps you on the right cheek, do not hide the left one, offer it instead, but jus' to divert your aggressor's attention and strike him dead. If anyone wants to sue you and take your shirt, beat him till he falls apart and then throw him into a well. And if someone forces you to do somethin' 'gainst your will, stab his heart and send him to hell. You shouldn't love your enemies, but hate them instead and feel damn glad when you know they're dead. In the bottom of your heart, the will to kill'em must always remain strong cos only fools love those who do them wrong."

*by JESUS

INCONVENIENT COMMENTS

"In the Bible it reads that Jesus said: 'And truly I say to you that it's easier for a camel to go thru the eye of a needle than for a rich man to enter the kingdom of God.' However, there's no way to know if he really said these words, for the Greek writer who wrote them wasn't present writing down Jesus' words on that occasion. Therefore, he just imagined Jesus had said those words. So, Jesus may well have said to the crowd: 'It's easier for a rich man to go thru the eye of a needle riding a donkey while smoking pot than for a poor man to enter the cage of a monkey called Scott." *(laughs)*

"As Jesus was walking beside the Sea of Galilee, he saw two fishers, they were called Ephraim and Zachariah, nicknamed Zach – the bible says they were "br<u>oth</u><u>ers</u>", but in fact they were "<u>l</u><u>overs</u>" *(laughs)*. This mistake was caused by a mistranslation." *(laughs)*

*by SETH THE JOKER, ONE OF JESUS' FIVE APOSTLES

GOD AND THE COW

"In India they venerate the cow..." (continued on page 69)

*by SETH THE JOKER, ONE OF JESUS' FIVE APOSTLES

HE WILL NEVER COME BACK

"Christians, whether they're straight or gay..." (continued on page 70)

*by SETH THE JOKER, ONE OF JESUS' FIVE APOSTLES

A LOGICAL CONCLUSION

"I wonder why some people for lack of logical reasoning insist on saying that Jesus was black. Don't they watch TV? You see, all Jews shown on it are white, therefore it means that there aren't black Jews in Israel.

You see, if it's like this nowadays when it's so easy to fly from one country to another, just imagine how it was in Jesus' time. So, it's easy to conclude that back then the Jews didn't even know black people existed.

Well, be that as it may, it can logically be concluded that since Jesus was Jew he was white too – though in fact, he was a half-breed. Since, you see, he actually was born as a result of the rape committed by a Roman soldier against his mother. By the way, that soldier's name was Tiberius Julius Abdes Pantera.

Anyway, it does not matter the color of your skin or the stink of your fart. What really matters is the love you got within your heart." *(laughs)*

*by CONFUCIUS, CHINESE PHILOSOPHER, 551-479 BC

FOLLOWING JESUS' EXAMPLE

"I think it's unfair to bash the evangelical pastors who get rich off the money donated by the gullible believers that attend their churches. The fact is that pastors should be admired instead, for they are remarkable skillful masters of sophistic rhetoric and, therefore, owners of great persuasive power. They're a bizarre mix of hypnotists-psychologists-sellers-lecturers. It's important to highlight that the believers give them money willingly and gladly. You see, apart from that, they use their rhetorical power to do good both for them and for their minions.

It's interesting to note that they provide a relevant service to society by rescuing many people from the criminal world and preventing many young people from engaging in crime thru the power of their speech, which is fully based on Jesus's teachings – you see, such a fact occurs mainly in third world countries like Brazil, for example. Just for the record, they never teach people to do bad deeds.

It's also interesting to note that the Bible is kinda like their manual and so, consequently, Jesus is their source of inspiration, for he did something somewhat similar to pay us, his apostles, so that we worked as his pitchmen advertising his alleged divine healing powers. I mean, he cleverly devised an efficient commercial scheme that provided him with an easy living without having to work hard as he did in his younger years back in Egypt, his birthplace. You see, politicians are the ones who, in fact, deserve bashing, for they steal the tax money people are obliged to give through the taxes they have to pay."

On another note, I feel I must point out that I'm an atheist despite my favorable view of evangelical pastors, strange as it may seem.

*by EPHRAIM, ONE OF JESUS' FIVE APOSTLES

SMARTER THAN JESUS

"In the following text, you're going to see that not only some letters of the title Jesus was given are equal to the ones of the first name of a certain underdog called Charles Manson. You see, I deem it important to highlight that he was just half good and half bad like ev'rybody else. He sure was no angel, but he wasn't the devil either. On second thought, he was an angel only if compared to Hitler. Just kidding. *(laughs)* Well, the previously mentioned letters are in the title "**CHRiSt**" and in the name "**CHaRleS**".

For fuck's sake, he was just a former conman, petty thief and pimp – in fact, he was only an unfairly convicted imp *(laughs)*.

Well, I also deem it important to point out that the surname "MANSON" is somewhat the inverted form of the appositive phrase "SON OF MAN", which Jesus used several times to refer to himself. Oddly enough, even their stories have some rather remote weird slight similarities: you see, just like Jesus he was an only child, though the Bible says he had siblings, which isn't true – I mean, I can affirm this cos I went to his late grandparents' house many times and, so, I know his mother had no other child but him.

In addition to that, as he was her only child she had a very tender connection with him so much so that she even called him by an affectionate nickname, namely **Shushu**, derived from his name Ye**shu**a – though he was already a bearded grown man *(laughs)*. Btw, this nickname is similar to the French word "chouchou", meaning "dear/ my dear/ darling /honey". It's pronounced as "shoushou" with the stress on the second syllable. In order to get information about it, search for the article entitled "chouchu / French to English", published on the internet by "Proz.com" on 10/14/2003.

You see, like Jesus he had a Mary too – the surname of his Mary was Brunner and the one of Jesus' was Magdalene. By the way, I must point out that Charlie, as his friends used to call him, put a baby in his Mary, but Jesus didn't put one in his. Hell, it's a wonder that he hasn't put any baby in her belly – well, maybe he performed some kind of miracle not to let her get pregnant *(laughs)* – just kidding. You see, the only explanation I can find for such a fact is that he was sterile, though actually not even he knew that.

Be that as it may, that little rascal surely was smarter than Jesus, for instead of brutish ugly fishermen, he gathered as apostles mostly lots of kind horny girls – most of them pretty ones. Moreover, that naughty little dude even slept with all of them, but only if Jesus was crazy he would sleep with any one of his apostles *(laughs)*.

And, to top it all off, Tex Watson, one of his casual male followers, was sorta like his Judas, or rather his Jed[1], and the DA[2] in charge of his case was kinda like his Pontius Pilate – but unlike this Roman governor, that scumbag didn't wash his hands cos he had bad hygiene habits *(laughs)*. You see, I think it's also relevant to point out that Manson even looked a bit like Jesus back in the sixties.

By the way, it's also important to highlight the fact that while Jesus used weed as a basic ingredient to prepare a potion to heal the sick, Manson used it to smoke *(laughs)*. Ah, before I forget, Jesus and he had an outstanding thing in common: both were kinda like anti-heroes. Though Manson was in fact more like a social misfit, a hell-bent survivor in this crazy unfair world ruled by crooks.

You see, "anti-heroes are conflicted, flawed, complex characters who do not have the typical virtues, values and characteristics of traditional heroes. Though their actions are noble, it doesn't necessarily mean that they act for good reasons like conventional heroes. They have dark sides, hidden secrets and may even have a flawed moral code, but ultimately, they have good intentions."

On a related note, in order to get information on the subject of anti-heroes, search for the article entitled "Anti-hero: Definitions, Meaning & Examples of Characters", published on the internet by "StudySmarter UK" – and to get information about the fact that Jesus used weed to heal the sick, search for the article entitled "BBC NEWS / Health/ Cannabis linked to Biblical healing", published on the internet by BBC on 01/06/03.

Well, to cap it all off, you see, in the same way that Jesus once saved Mary Magdalene from being stoned, Charles Manson also saved Luella, Tex Watson's girlfriend, not from being stoned, but from being raped and killed by a certain drug dealer called Bernard Lotsapoppa Crowe – you know, Manson even shot him but he escaped alive cos Charlie wasn't a good shot *(laughs)*. Speaking of the devil, Tex Watson was a psychopathic petty drug dealer – a casual member of Charlie's commune, who had ripped off that drug dealer previously mentioned. That's why he kept Tex's girlfriend prisoner so that he could get his money back, but it's obvious that he intended to kill her and Tex even if he returned his money – something that Tex wouldn't do for sure – and in fact never did. *(laughs)*.

It's noteworthy that just like Jesus he was framed, didn't have a fair trial and was convicted without being guilty. And as if that weren't enough, he was accused of brainwashing his folks and send them to kill, but it's sheer bullshit, for this brainwashing stuff ain't real – such a bullshit sure was made up. You see, though he was portrayed by the mainstream media as a serial killer, he actually never killed anyone, or rather, he once killed – a hen *(laughs)* and even pleaded guilty to this crime in an interview. *(laughs)*

Well, afterwards, in prison, it turned out that he wasn't actually a monster, a real-life boogeyman or evil incarnate, but just a clownlike old man that made grimaces and uttered clever, weird, puzzling comments.

You see, after being "crucified", Jesus became the central figure of the largest religion in the world and people devotedly worship him. But Charles Manson, the underdog, on the contrary, was changed into the personification of evil by the mainstream media and most people celebrated his death.

Fact is that, unfortunately, out of pure sadism, heaven's board of directors must have decided that such a poor devil –laughably and wrongly labeled as "the most dangerous man in the world", should be born to be an underdog in this unfair crazy shitty world." *(laughs)*

[1] The name of the guy who betrayed Jesus was "Jed" and not Judas as it's said in the bible – this fact is explained by the apostle Seth further on up this book.

[2] DA: District Attorney.

*by SETH THE JOKER, ONE OF JESUS' FIVE APOSTLES

CAUGHT RED-HANDED

"Jesus stood up for the poor and for the downtrodden as well as for prostitutes and women convicted of adultery. He was always on the side of the weaker ones stricken by injustice, hypocrisy and prejudice. You bet if gays had already come out of the closet back in his day – when people were as biased as hell, he'd surely defend them as well.

You see, Herod himself was also a closeted gay and felt madly attracted to his brawny soldiers. It was really hard for him to repress his homosexual impulses.

You see, I deem important to highlight that, apart from me, Jesus prevented some adulteresses and prostitutes from being stoned. Well, speaking of which, I must point out that I wasn't a prostitute, contrary to the popular belief. What happened was that some 5 centuries later a certain screwy pope, off the top of his head, decided to proclaim that I was one, and his version of me was popularized from then on.

Well, I mean, I just cheated on my husband cos he was a damn toxic abusive bastard. So, out of emotional needs I sought consolation and pleasure in the bed of another man. But sadly, I was caught red-handed by that motherfucker.

Anyway, in fact, something good came out of that distressing situation after all, cos Jesus, my hero, rescued me and I was unofficially named by him as kinda like one of his apostles and permanent lover too."
(laughs)

*by MARY MAGDALENE, JESUS' UNOFFICIAL APOSTLE AND PERMANENT LOVER

THE BAD GOOD FRIDAY

"Ev'ry Good Friday Christians re-enact the Way of the Cross, holy shit, but it's just another mistake they commit, though they cannot see it. They cannot understand that Jesus would only be pleased indeed, if the money they spent was given to the ones in need.

Yet, they throw lots of money away on the staging of this shit, though it didn't happen as told in this so-called Holy Writ."

*by MARY MAGDALENE, JESUS' UNOFFICIAL APOSTLE AND PERMANENT LOVER

GOD VS. THE BIG BANG

"Did God create the universe all by himself, with his gang or was it created by the Big Bang?

None of the options above, for God is just a mythological character and his gang is composed by mythological characters as well, so they couldn't have created anything, holy hell! The Big Bang, on the other hand, is also another far-fetched implausible theory devised by man – a creature fucking perverse, in his stupid useless attempt to explain the origin of the universe.

Well, the universe just exists, the same way as the sun and the moon. It surely was not created by no imaginary buffoon. The idea stating that ev'rything needs to be created was conceived by man – who's by the way, God's creator, contrary to what they say. Even though believers cannot accept it, for their heads are full of shit."

*by SETH THE JOKER, ONE OF JESUS' FIVE APOSTLES

MOTHER NATURE'S CODE NAME

Atheists are dead wrong, for God is real – Christians are not insane. You see, God is just Mother Nature's code name.

Moreover, God is not man's creator, it's not like this. In fact, Mother Earth is his real creatress. I mean, man can unworriedly exist without God forever and a day, but God can't exist without man in anyway – whether they're straight or gay. Well, to confirm this statement, you must remember that the American Indians didn't know anything about the white man's God and his alleged power before his arrival in the Mayflower – however, they were happy, wild and free and just lived off the land like it should be...

But their white foe brought his God to them, not trapped in a bottle but in the Bible – and along with him, their ruin.

JESUS AND KARL MARX

Strange as it may seem, Jesus already kinda came back, but in an unfairly detracted sorta warped historical figure whose name was Karl Marx. Oddly enough, he was a Jew too, for though he was born in Germany his parents were Jews. So, ethnically he was a Jew as well. His father managed to change his own name from Herschel Mordechai to Heinrich Marx and abandoned his Jewish faith to escape anti-Semitism.

Note that Karl is the Germanic form of the English name Charles. So, the English form of his name has some letters in common with Jesus' title, namely Christ – as can be seen as follows: **CH**a**R**le**S** – **CHR**i**S**t.

Then, in 1848, together with his friend Friedrich Engels, who was kinda like his only apostle, he wrote "The Communist Manifesto" – a kind of doctrine that idealized a fair fraternal egalitarian society. But, sadly, 34 years after his death, those money-grubbing motherfucking Bolsheviks, who created the URSS, coopted his doctrine and implemented it in an oppressive distorted way – you bet your ass he must still be rolling over in his grave because of it *(laughs)*.

Next, those motherfucking Bolsheviks shrewdly and evilly managed to spread it to some other countries and it turned out to be even kinda worse than capitalism itself – in the end, capitalism turned out to be the lesser of two evils.

JESUS IN HIS OWN WORDS (cont.)

"**I**'ve decided to write this book with my friend Sam for three reasons: the first one was to have fun, after all ev'ryone needs a break 'cause life ain't no piece of cake *(laughs)*. The second was to clarify some main misconceptions about my story, which was rather ordinary and deprived of glory – and the third was to show the believers and ev'ryone else I'm something of a **holy ghost**writer myself (*laughs*).

You see, one thing that I do really insist on saying unto thee is that there was nothing holy about me. I was just another ordinary guy like any other under the sky just waiting around to die – well, on second thought, in fact, I was way shrewder than ev'rybody else, even if I do say so myself. *(laughs)* Besides being a mixed-race Roman-Jew taller than most other Jews too.

Well, ev'ry Christian believes that my father was God and that my stepdad was a poor old carpenter named Joe, but it ain't so; besides, I don't even believe in God, you know. I mean, as a matter of fact, truly, truly I say to you that my real father in that era was a Roman soldier called Tiberius Julius Abdes Pantera[1].

You see, I inherited his fair skin – a bit weathered by walking under the Middle East burning sun, plus predominantly European facial features and height: I was 5'7" tall just like him, while the male Jew's average height was 5'5" at that time – a slight but considerable difference.

He had blondish hair and pale blue eyes, but my hair and eyes were dark brown like the ones of my mother – besides, I also had a dark brown beard. You see, it's kind of interesting to point out that I usually tried to keep both my hair and beard trimmed when I was in town.

By the way, you can get information about this soldier in the book entitled "The Jesus Dynasty" by Tabor, James – published by "Simon & Schuster" on 05/04/2006 and in the following articles published on the internet: "What did Jesus do?" by Adam Gopnik, published by "The New Yorker" on 05/17/2010, "Celsus as quoted by Origen", published by "Early Christian Writings", "Origen – Celsus' Objections to Christianity", published by "Early Church Texts" and "Celsus *vs* the Early Christians", published by "Street Apologist" on 11/01/2014.

As for my mother, she was a 12-year-old pretty country girl who, against her will, married that previously mentioned old carpenter called Joe, cos her father obliged her to do so; for that lewd elderly guy paid him way more than he could ask for. But, contrary to what they say in the Bible, old bawdy Joe was nothing poor – in fact, he was a moneyed boor.

You know, back in my day, a father was allowed to sell his daughter when he was in need, cos, back then, a daughter was considered just an ordinary part of his assets indeed. That's why my grandfather sold my mother to that toxic old raunchy scumbag... so, on getting married, my poor beloved mother felt like a helpless bird caught in a trap...

Btw, in order to get information about the status of daughters in ancient Jewish Law, search for the Bible excerpt of "Exodus 21:7- 11 that reads: "And if a man sells his daughter to be a female slave, she shall not go out as the male slaves do. If she does not please her master, who has betrothed her to himself, then he shall let her be redeemed...", published on the internet by "Bible.com". Besides, search also for the article entitled "Slavery in Judaism", published on the internet by "Jewish Virtual Library" as well.

On a related note, in order to know more about the age of my mother when she was bought, search for the article entitled "Was Mary 12 and Joseph 90 years old when they married?", published on the internet by "Graced Follower". Well, they exaggerated as for old Joe's age, for the life span back then was very short. So, on average, people didn't even reach the age of 50. In fact, old Joe was an exception to the rule and was 60, but a man his age back then was already too old. Thus, he practically had one foot in the grave when he bought my poor beloved mother *(laughs)*....

Nevertheless, my beloved mother was really 12, for, you see, back then, according to the Jewish Law, a father could sell his daughter to make money when in need. But only after she had his first period, which usually occurred at the age of 12. Because if the girl didn't menstruate, she wouldn't be able to bear children and so she didn't have commercial value.

But not ev'rything went right for Joe cos, due to old age, he didn't have a proper performance in bed, which drove him mad... and so he couldn't get her pregnant – not even by God's decree, which pissed him off deeply...

Well, thus, it happened that on a certain day this soldier Pantera managed to coax her into getting laid and then I was made. However, his error was not to keep his damn mouth shut; after all, he was a soldier of the Roman army and should behave respectfully toward the Jewish womenfolk, chiefly toward married women. You see, this behavior pattern was part of a tacit agreement made between the Romans and the Jewish authority at that time, after they established their rule over Palestine. Then, he was kicked out of the army and forced into exile in Germany. You see, in fact, he wasn't kicked out of the army just for raping my beloved naughty naïve mother – though this fact must have triggered such a decision, but mainly because he had a problematic military record.

Btw, you can get more information about Pantera's exile in the article entitled "What did Jesus do?", published on the internet by "The New Yorker" on 05/17/2010 and in the book entitled "The Jesus Dynasty" by Tabor, James – published by "Simon & Schuster" on 05/04/2006.

Well, when her pregnancy started becoming noticeable, Joe became a bit suspicious, so she shrewdly made up that far-fetched meant-for-duping-fools angel story... in the beginning he swallowed her big fat lie, but it didn't take that long for him to realize she was fooling him... so, not to be stoned as an adulteress, she stole some cash from his stash and managed to flee to Egypt along with a merchant caravan...

therefore, in fact, she didn't ride a donkey but rather a camel while carrying me in her womb. *(laughs)*

On a somewhat related note, I must also point out that the far-fetched story about the star of Bethlehem and the magi was interpolated in the Bible to add a mystical aura to my story. You see, according to "Dictionary.com", interpolation is the process of altering a text by the insertion of new matter, especially, deceptively or without authorization. Btw, a perfect example of interpolation is the one that a certain Christian made about me in a text by Flavius Josephus – its obvious goal was to make him bear witness to my existence. Btw, in order to know more about the topic of interpolation, search for the article entitled "Interpolations in the New Testament", published on the internet by "The Christian Classics Ethereal Library" on 03/10/ 2023. Besides, search for the one entitled "You use Josephus' quote about Jesus in your book..." published on the internet by "Evidence for Christianity" on 08/07/2013 as well.

So, I was born not very far from the famous pyramids in a house where my mother worked as a maidservant in exchange for food and shelter. By the way, I don't know the exact year, month or day of my birth, cos at that time there wasn't a systematized birth registration system aimed at ev'ryone like nowadays. So, how on earth do they say that I was born on December 25?

Anyway, time went by and when I grew up I started working as a carpenter, but in between times I managed to learn the art of illusion and hypnotism, besides becoming an apothecary afterwards. Later, in order to gain more knowledge about all this stuff I spent some time in India. Then, I went to Greece to learn philosophy and sophistic rhetoric so that I could master the art of preaching and, therefore, develop skills to influence others and achieve my goals.

Thus, after spending about two years abroad, on a certain spring day, I returned and took my beloved mother along with me back to Palestine

– not to Israel, cos such a country didn't exist back in my day, since the State of Israel was created by the UN only after the Second World War.

You see, when I was born Romans ruled the Mediterranean area known as Palestine, modern day Israel, where I lived for about 3 years and a half after coming back from Egypt, my birthplace. By the way, to get information about the topic mentioned in the previous paragraph, search for the article entitled "First Century Palestine", published on the internet by "SWCS.com.au".

Well, to be more precise, I took her back to the rural area where my grandparent's house was located near the town of Gennesaret. You see, some time after arriving there, thru hypnotism and magic tricks, I managed to make five ignorant gullible fishermen believe I was the son of God and then they became my apostles – btw, according to the "Collins Dictionary", an apostle is someone who strongly believes in a particular philosophy, policy or cause and works hard to promote it. Well, in fact, in order to reach my goals, I subliminally hired those poor devils as sorta like my marketers to advertise my "divine" healing powers and then we went from city to city...

Btw, besides being my apostles they were also kinda like my bodyguards; because there were lots of thieves and robbers in all the cities – always ready to attack you specially at night. Not to mention the bullies, always ready to attack at any time. And to top it all off, there were lots of bandit gangs that attacked travelers in the wilderness, given that the Roman law enforcement system back then was only less sloppy than the Haitian one. *(laughs)* That's why through a hypnotic command I made my apostles able to use swords, spears and javelins skillfully to protect me and the money collected from the healings I performed, since I frequently traveled thru remote desolate areas to carry out my health care services. Apart from that, you see, I subliminally commanded them to help me stage some of my magic tricks, so they did it without really having awareness of what they did. That is, like all the other people they really believed I was the son of God. But, you see, most magic tricks I'd rather perform on my own, since I was so good at the art of illusion that I was able to deceive even myself. *(laughs)* Especially because I mixed magic tricks with hypnotism.

Furthermore, back then, you see, walking the streets late at night without the protection of armed guards in most parts of Jerusalem, as well as in most parts of other Palestinian cities and towns such as Bethlehem, Sepphoris and Hebron, for example, meant signing one's own death warrant. The same could be said about most foreign cities and towns such as Rmaych in Lebanon, located near the border with Palestine, for example – where I once went to heal a rich man who sent for me so that I could heal him and paid me lots of money for my healing service, which, by the way, really restored his health...

You see, living was so dangerous like that cos people back then, such as Arabs, Samaritans, Jews and Persians, for example, were almost as bloodthirsty, dangerous, warlike and greedy as folks are nowadays.

I think I should point out that my apostles didn't carry weapons when we were in town during the day, cos the Romans didn't allow Jewish civilians to carry weapons, for they saw it as a potential threat to their dominion – but, at night, it was a different story, because, as they say, at night all cats are grey and they were even greyer back in my day *(laughs)*.

Thus, on arriving in a certain city my apostles started advertising my alleged amazing healing powers around it. While spreading the word that I was the son of God and could work miracles and heal all kinds of diseases. They did so in order to arouse people's curiosity and interest, cos, back then, folks were way more religious, superstitious and gullible than nowadays – that's why they could be so easily duped. *(laughs)*

So, putting into practice all I had learned (and that was improved by me later – to the point of even kinda leading me to believe I really had acquired supernatural powers) *(laughs)* I worked miracles, or better said, I performed magic tricks while healing the sick through therapeutic energy transmission and hypnotism, that is, by means of suggestive healing, which led those ignorant Jews to believe I really was the son of God – besides, I also relied on the help of an herbal cure-all devised by me, which had hemp and black cumin as its basic ingredients. Speaking of which, black cumin has been used as a medicinal plant for thousands of years – you see, back in my day, people said jokingly it could heal ev'rything except ugliness *(laughs)*. You see, to find more information about black cumin, search for the article entitled "Black Cumin", published on the internet by the "Maharishi Ayurveda Health Center".

Anyway, no matter how irrelevant it may seem, I think it's necessary to highlight that I never healed anybody through the use of spittle and mud as it is written in John 9:6-7. *(laughs)* You see, I must also mention that the fake resurrections I performed were accomplished by hypnotizing the people who were summoned by my apostles. Thank God those shows of "divine" power manifestation prompted them to donate me more money, because those ignorant gullible superstitious people believed that they would be rewarded by God if they did so – and also cos they needed to have their diseases healed, for they realized I was the best healer they had ever seen. This way, I went about making a living without having to work hard like most ordinary people.

On another note, not long afterwards, I hired 2 of my permanent followers of Jerusalem to help my apostles protect me and the money coming from the healing sessions I performed – chiefly during my travels thru the wilderness. Btw, I deem it important to highlight that I instilled hypnotic commands into their minds as well so that they became able to use weapons skillfully too. You see, I also deem necessary to point out that I paid them a salary that was worth less than half of what I paid each of my apostles – but even so it was a quite good salary at that time. Besides, they also helped to advertise my "divine" healing powers – which helped to increase the daily cash inflow.

By the way, I performed magic tricks to add a mystical aura to the healings I performed so that people thought I really had divine powers.

You know, during my healing performances Uriah played the lyre and, sometimes, sang – by the way, he had such a pleasing soothing voice.

In the meantime, Elijah and Aaron, two of my followers, managed the people seeking medical care and Seth received the money they paid, while Ephraim and Zach handled the sheep people gave in exchange for the healings when they didn't have cash. Then, inside the room Jed helped me with the sick... Meanwhile, out there, as soon as the sheep were gathered, they took them to the market to be sold.

This activity provided me with good money to make a living without having to work hard like most people. Not to mention the money my apostles and followers collected from the crowd during the sermons I preached as well – occasions in which I performed some amazing healings and magic tricks, viewed as miracles by the people – besides carrying out some fake resurrections by means of hypnotism and illusion.

By the way, during my healing sessions the "ketoret", which had "kannabus"* and myrrh as its basic ingredients, was burned filling the room with a pleasant soothing smell and creating a harmonious peaceful atmosphere. Btw, the "ketoret" was a blend of herbs and balms, which, when burned, released fragrant smoke. Btw, you can find more information about the "ketoret" in the article entitled "Ketoret – Chassidic Masters – Parshah", published on the internet by "Chabad.org".

On a related note, to get information about the herb called "kannabus", mentioned in the previous paragraph, search for the article entitled "Jesus Christ used cannabis?", published on the internet by SakshiZion.com on 01/19/20.

Furthermore, I think you may be interested to know that ancient Israelites burned cannabis as part of their religious rituals, according to a certain archeological study. You see, to find more information about this subject, search for the article entitled "Cannabis burned during worship by ancient Israelites – study", published on the internet by BBC on 05/29/20.

Well, I also think it's somewhat interesting to point out that when we traveled from city to city to carry out my health care services I and my staff didn't go on foot, but rather riding camels cos we used to travel long distances, sometimes thru the desert, and camels are fitter than horses to carry out that function.

On a somewhat related note, I want to make clear that contrary to what they say in the Bible I never entered Jerusalem riding no donkey. In fact, my staff and I entered that city riding camels. Besides, I didn't go there to celebrate the Passover, for I didn't give a damn about religious celebrations and stuff like that. In reality, I went there just to perform my healings and magic tricks, which were seen as miracles by the crowd – and, as usual, collect some money before traveling to another city.

Apart from that, they also wrote that I once entered the temple, overturned the tables of the money changers and the benches of the merchants driving them out while saying: "My house will be called a house of prayer, but you have made it a den of robbers." Well, this fact never happened, for I never entered that damn temple, given that those malicious spiteful envious temple priests hated me, cos they viewed me as a kind of competitor that was taking away most of the templegoers along with the

money they donated. Besides, I was an atheist and didn't waste my time on this stupid useless stuff of house of prayer and things like that.

On another note, I also think you may be interested to know that I always defended the weaker ones – the poor and downtrodden, from the injustices perpetrated by their fellowmen. Well, I did it by hypnotizing their aggressors in a way that they saw ferocious lions instead of their victims and ran away scared to death *(laughs)*.

Moreover, I also prevented some prostitutes and women convicted of adultery from being stoned. In those occasions I hypnotized the angry city dwellers and instilled a hypnotic command into their minds so that instead of their preys they saw giant snakes spitting fire and ran away terrified, besides becoming unable to see them from then on.

Aside from that, they wrote that to save a certain woman who, by the way, was Mary Magdalene, I said, "He that is without sin among you, let him first cast a stone at her." But it ain't true, you see, what really happened was that I stood in front of the furious crowd, drew a dividing line on the ground between them and me – with one the stones they had thrown at her – and uttered the magical word "abracadabra" disorderedly, which turned into "rabadabarac", then I counted to five and *voilà*! The magic happened! Next, those damned, smelly, hypocritical vipers rushed away in fear and she became invisible to them afterwards. You see, if I had just stood in front of the crowd speaking those words they say I spoke, those stupid angry people would have stoned me together with her – simple as that.

Btw, "abracadabra" is a magical word based on the Kabbalistic tradition meaning something nearly like "I will create from nothing as I speak". To get more information about such a word, search for the article entitled "Abracadabra! Is that Hebrew?", published on the internet by aleteia.org on 09/07/2016.

Well, I know it may seem too simplistic, far-fetched and kind of stupid now, but what matters is that it worked perfectly well in all occasions at that time. Maybe because people back then were such a superstitious ignorant gullible bunch of morons. You know, I always did it to instill hypnotic commands into people's minds whenever it was necessary or convenient for me.

You see, I feel I must also point out that I uttered the word "abracadabra" disorderedly to stand out from the several other miracle makers back then, who also used this magical word to cast their fake magic spells. You see, I dare to say I was the only one of them who wasn't a mere charlatan – even if I do say so myself. *(laughs)*

I mean, Mary committed no crime; she just cheated on her husband, a toxic sexist scumbag like the overwhelming majority of husbands back then. Poor thing, she was abused by him and was needy, so she found consolation and pleasure in the bed of another man. But sadly, she was caught red-handed by that wretch. *(laughs)*

In addition, I feel I must point out that after saving her I didn't say, "Neither do I condemn you. Go and sin no more." In fact, I just unofficially named her as kinda like one of my apostles and permanent lover *(laughs)*.

On an unrelated note, Christians wonder why I didn't write down any text or letter for posterity; but the answer is easy: I didn't do it because I couldn't care less, for all I really wanted was to go about my healthcare business while making money to keep my "miracles" and healings company running smoothly – so that it could provide me with an easy living. Anyway, verily I say unto thee that ye can get more information about this subject in a text entitled "Did Jesus write anything?", published on the internet by "Blue Letter Bible".

By the way, I know you would like me to speak about the Last Supper, but it ain't possible: just because it didn't happen. In fact, I spent that night with Hannah, a beautiful, childless, rich widow and one of my casual lovers. Verily I say unto you that we drank lots of wine, but thank God it wasn't my blood, cos I don't like how it tastes, for I ain't no vampire *(laughs)*.

You see, the account of the Last Supper was just another blatant interpolation. You know, I wonder how people can be so gullible to the point of believing that far-fetched story saying that I knew Judas, or rather Jed[2], would betray me – Lord, I was a magician and not a clairvoyant *(laughs)*. Besides, if I knew that rascal would snitch on me, it's obvious that I would have fired him long before he did it.

On a different note, they wrongly say in John 2:4 that I disrespectfully spoke to my mother: "Woman, what have I to do with thee: my time has not yet come..." But it is absolutely untrue, cos I truly loved and respected all good-hearted women, especially my beloved mother whom I loved and respected even more than I loved and respected myself.

Some scholars say I was an Essene; but it ain't true, for I regarded them as just a bunch of religious bigoted wackos that lived in the desert foolishly studying the Torah, fasting, praying and performing stupid useless purification rituals. The only thing I admired about them was the fact that they lived in a kind of ancient communism, in which all possessions were collectively owned. But the main reason why I always stayed away from them was that they excluded women from their community.

Well, judging by their aversion towards women, I think they were just a damn bunch of weird misogynistic gay religious lunatics. As for me, I have always regarded kind-hearted women as lovely beings that should always be loved and worshiped. But it has to be noted that only kind-hearted women must always be loved and worshiped, for the evil-hearted ones are the devil himself and as I also developed the ability of reading people's minds, I always kept away from them. You see, you can find detailed information about the Essenes in the article entitled "Essene, Dead Sea Scrolls", published on the internet by "Britannica" on 09/27/23.

Changing the subject, to be honest, I avoided performing "miracles" and healings in the town of Gennesaret, since it was located very near the rural area where my mother was born, for it upset me to overhear some mean people, mostly the elderly, gloatingly and mockingly, call me "Yeshu ben Pantera" (Jesus son of Pantera) and also "Yeshu ben stada" (Jesus, son of the adulteress) – I was called like that cos they knew my mother committed adultery with this Roman soldier nicknamed Pantera and that he was my real father. Btw, you can find more information about the previous topic in the article entitled "X-The Talmud ben Stada – Jesus Stories", published on the internet by "The Gnosis Archives", adapted from the book "The Talmud ben Stada – Jesus Stories" by Mead, G. R. S. – published by "Kessinger Publishing" on 12/08/2005.

On a somewhat related note, I deem it important to highlight that the name Yeshua (that is, my name) was maliciously and shrewdly changed by those damn hypocritical nasty temple priests into Yesh**u** – by just dropping the final "a" of my name, they somehow coined a new one meaning something nearly as "the unworthy cursed trickster", which carried a damn negative connotation. Then, they made sure that this damn new name attributed to me was known by most people. By doing so, those mean bigoted pharisaical bastards played a malicious trick on me.

Their evil action kind of tainted my reputation and some Jews among the poor also started viewing me as a deceiver. You see, the temple priests, those damn scumbags, did it about 1 year and a half after my return to Palestine; but, fortunately, most of the poor still kept believing in my "divine" powers and continued giving me money to pay for my healing services, instead of going to the temple to pray for God's help in vain.

So that you can find more information regarding the previous topic search for the text entitled "The Jewish Jesus' story: Toledot Yeshu", by Eli Yassif, published on the internet by "Tablet Magazine" on 12/23/16. Besides, search also for and for the one entitled "Yeshua or Yeshu" – What does it mean?", also published on the internet by "Jews for Jesus" on 03/01/08 as well.

On a related note, in short, the "Sefer Toledot Yeshu" (The Book of Jesus' life) is an ancient Jewish text that somewhat tells the real story of my life, though in a rather scornful and distorted way – showing an off-the-wall unbigoted perspective. You see, it's considered profane and uncertified by the Roman Catholic Church 'cause, from among the texts about my life, the Romans selected only the ones that could fit their interests, besides manipulating part of them.

Well, they shrewdly coopted the parts of the story of my life that suited them best, plus the Jewish mythology, in order to create a powerful religion to dominate people through fear rather than by the sword. That's why they dismiss the "Sefer toledot Yeshu" as just an ancient scornful tale of my life – but it's not so scornful like that. In fact, it's somewhat revealing and bears a certain rather weird remote closeness to reality, though it's undeniably, blatantly and extremely biased, derisive and twisted.

I also think it's important to highlight that the name Y**eshu**, somehow, gave origin to the moniker **eshu** – a trickster God of the Youruba people of Nigeria, Africa. By the way, you can find more information about this subject in the article entitled "Eshu", published on the internet by "Encyclopedia.com".

You see, it's relevant to mention that most middle-class citizens, most nobles, most rich people and all of the temple priests plus just a few people among the poor also called me derisively "Jesus the outlaw". Because I sometimes hung out with prostitutes, bandits and tricksters drinking wine and preaching in the taverns, besides healing and performing magic tricks, which they gullibly believed to be miracles like all other people out there. You see, there were lots of other miracle makers like me back in my day – though I was the best of all, even if I do say so myself. *(laughs)*

Well, while we are on the subject of miracle makers, I think I should also mention John the Baptist, a wacko who was a well-known preacher that roamed the area of the Jordan River – though he wasn't in fact a miracle maker, but just a poor delusional weirdo who really believed in ancient prophecies, angels, God and all that stuff. He lived in the wilderness, wore clothes of camel's hair and ate chiefly honey and grasshoppers – to say the least. *(laughs)*

You see, in the Bible they say he was a cousin of mine, but, in fact, we were no relatives. They wrote he was my cousin due to a mistranslation made while the New Testament was translated from Greek to Latin. In case you want to find more information about the topic of the Bible translation from Greek into Latin, search for the article entitled "Saint Jerome: The Perils of a Bible Translator", published on the internet by "Saint Mary's press" in 2023.

On a somewhat related note, it's obvious that my apostles didn't write the gospels attributed to them, for they were all brutish illiterate fishermen – and, to make things even worse, the New Testament started being written about 70 years after my death; but back in my day the average life span was quite short due chiefly to poor nutrition and bad hygiene habits, entailing various diseases, which were aggravated by the lack of healthcare. So, nobody could live that long, even if the person was holy like they said I was *(laughs)*. By the way, healthcare in Palestine back then was far worse than it is in Somalia nowadays. So, how the hell could any one of my apostles live for so long? And to top it all off, the New Testament was written in Greek!

This leads me to ask: if they could barely speak their own language properly and were illiterate fishermen, how would they be able to write in Greek, a very difficult language to master even nowadays that there are efficient learning tools, which weren't even dreamed of back in those days?

Now, speaking again of that lunatic preacher called John the Baptist; you see, when I heard about that wacko I had the insight that he could well be useful for me to reach my goals. So, by means of illusion and hypnotism, I led him to believe I was really the son of God and then he gladly baptized me. From then on, he started spreading the word that I was indeed the son of God, which urged many more people to give me money and, thus, contribute towards my easy living.

Meanwhile, lots of people started leaving the temple and resorting to my healing services, among whom there were many middle-class citizens some nobles and several rich people who gladly paid good money for my health care services, besides resorting to them frequently – which made me real glad for sure, cos it meant more money coming in to keep my "miracles" and healings company running even more smoothly.

So, those spiteful money-grubbing temple priests started getting worried 'cause they were too greedy and felt like they were losing money, for many templegoers were trading them for me and ceasing to make donations. Even though people were obliged by the Romans to pay a tax to the temple priests, for according to a deal made between them, they would support the Romans and in return would receive such a tax in order to support their lavish lifestyle. Btw, you can find more information about the previous topic in the book entitled "The Message and the Kingdom" by Horsley, Richard A. – published by "Fortress Press" in 2002.

Thus, those damn temple priests managed to get Jed to rat me out to the Romans. You see, that good-for-nothing scumbag told them I was inciting people to rebel against their authority – which wasn't quite true cos I just enlightened people about the oppression they were subjected to, though shrewdly and subliminally.

On a somewhat related note, once, when, by means of a parable, I was telling my apostles that I hadn't come to Earth to bring peace but rather a sword, a Zealot overheard and, thinking wrongly that I was preaching armed struggle, meddled in our conversation inviting me to join his warlike party, but I immediately turned down the invitation of that reckless rebellious fool.

And speaking of armed struggle, you see, I in fact didn't mean to plot no rebellion against the Romans, but rather lead people to organize a kind of general strike in order to ease their oppression. In no way I thought of breaking the law even if it was enforced by the Romans. You see, as I was no fool, I was always extremely careful with my words not to get in trouble with the law, cos if I did so I would jeopardize my easy living. That's why I used parables to transmit subliminal messages while going about making money.

Anyway, the Romans believed Jed and then I was arrested. Well, the rest of the story ev'rybody knows – that is, more or less, for I wasn't crucified on the type of cross that Christians believe I was, but rather on a T-shaped cross, cos during the Roman Empire in the Middle East criminals were executed on special "Egyptian" crosses – called "Tau Crosses", which looked like the letter "T", and not on those stereotyped crosses shown in the pics portraying my crucifixion. By the way, in order to get more information about the previous subject, search for the article entitled "14 Types of Ancient Christian Crosses", published on the internet by "OrthoChristian.com" on 09/30/2016.

Besides, I didn't carry any cross cos there was none to be carried, for the crosses on which the prisoners would be crucified were already fixed to the ground of the courtyard in front of Jerusalem temple, as it was the largest area inside that city; besides, it was a place where the prisoners could easily be seen by the city dwellers. Cos the main objective of the crucifixion was to serve as a deterrent.

Now, what really happened was that those damn bastards took me to that place late at night and after stripping off my clothes they tied and nailed my legs spread apart to that damn T-shaped cross. Next, they cut off my genitals and left me there hanging upside down bleeding all night long till the following morning, the time when people would gather to watch the macabre show propitiated by me and the other prisoners.

So, while we are still on the subject of my crucifixion, to be faithful to the truth, I must point out that this resurrection stuff was all shrewdly made up by my apostles – including Jed, that damn scumbag, cos my other apostles didn't know he had betrayed me, or rather, only his cousin Seth knew it, but he didn't snitch on him for personal reasons; so, that's why they didn't kick him out of my former company after I was crucified by the Romans.

Well, you see, they stole my body from the sepulcher so that people thought I resurrected for having divine powers – and to top it all off, those old rascals managed to spread the far-fetched story that the soldiers, standing guard outside my sepulcher, got scared to death at the sight of an angel that popped out of nowhere and got them paralyzed *(laughs)* – and what's even more unbelievable and mind-blowing is the fact that back then the superstitious, ignorant gullible people swallowed their big fat lie so easily – just like believers still do nowadays. *(laughs)* But contrary to what's written in the bible there were no soldiers guarding my tomb, for the Romans viewed me as just another petty miracle maker like lots of others who roamed that region. Anyway, those little rascals managed to dupe people into believing that there were two strong soldiers standing guard outside my sepulcher. *(laughs)*

Be that as it may, the fact is that my apostles just followed my example, so they are not to blame. They did so just to keep on making money off my name *(laughs)*. By the way, I deem it important to highlight that lots of articles related to this text I wrote can be found on umpteen sites on the Web."

[1]<u>Pantera</u>: Panther

[2]<u>Jed</u>: The name of Jesus' traitor was Jed and not Judas as it's said in the

Bible. This is explained by the apostle Seth further on up this book.

THE NAKED TRUTH

"Jesus Christ will never come back come sunshine or rain cos he's afraid of being crucified again. So, you better stop believing he'll come back once more, for such a thing just bullshit for sure.

This bullshit is as real as the story that the pope gets naked to play ping pong – poor Christians, they're fucking wrong."

* by Uriah, one of Jesus' five apostles.

CRUCIFIED UPSIDE DOWN

"Gullible Christians really believe that Jesus carried that fucking heavy cross, besides being brutally beaten, but it's not true – the biblical accounts are wrong and deceptive. So, I feel I must point out that it didn't happen the way it's written in the Bible.

Well, in fact, there wasn't this so-called sacred road. Moreover, he wasn't crucified on the Golgotha hill, because it was located about 2 miles outside Jerusalem walls. Besides, that hill was quite high and had a steep slope composed of a rugged rocky terrain difficult to climb.

Actually, he and the other convicts were taken to the courtyard in front of Jerusas* temple – late at night not to attract onlookers before the scheduled time.

So, on arriving at that place all the prisoners were stripped of their clothes and their legs were tied and nailed spread apart to crossbars of T-shaped crosses. It's interesting to point out that they were nailed right above the ankles – next, their genitals were cut off and they were left there hanging upside down bleeding stark naked despoiled of their family jewels[2] *(laughs).* Then, as usual, the following morning a huge crowd would gather to watch the macabre show propitiated by the prisoners crucified upside down – you see, the crucifixion main purpose was to serve as a deterrent.

In fact, you see, during the Roman Empire in the Middle East outlaws were executed on special "Egyptian" crosses – called "Tau Crosses", which looked like the letter "T", and not on stereotyped ones as it's shown in the pics portraying Jesus's crucifixion. By the way, in order to get more information about the previous subject, search for the article entitled "14 Types of Ancient Christian Crosses", published on the internet by "OrthoChristian.com" on 09/30/2016.

Well, those T-shaped crosses were about 7' tall while Jesus was 5'7", so he remained there hanging upside down only about 17" above the ground – the blood that leaked from his severed crotch[3] rolled down his face and formed a pool on the ground below his head – by the way, the government of Iran somehow has coopted this punitive approach; however, they don't use crosses, but rather cranes, besides they neither strip the criminals of their clothes nor cut off their genitals.

So, after they were crucified upside down, Roman soldiers guarded the place and didn't allow anybody to get near. People had to keep a certain distance from them till they began to stink, usually after 2 or 3 days. Then, they were taken away by their relatives – the prisoners that didn't have relatives were buried in paupers' graves. That's a summarized account of what really happened to Jesus."

*by GAIUS CORVINUS, ROMAN SOLDIER WHO HELPED TIE AND NAIL
JESUS TO THE CROSS

[1] Gaius: This name gave origin to the word "gay", meaning homosexual, for this soldier was gay and the homosexuality ingrained in his name, somehow, found a way to be reborn many centuries later.

[2] Slang for genitals.

[3] Slang for genitals.

*Jerusa: short for Jerusalem – in fact, that was how most people called that fuckin' shitty **sick city**. *(laughs)* Of course, it was pronounced *Yehusha* in Hebrew, because *Jerusa* is the way its shortened form is pronounced in English.

THE GREATEST MAGICIAN OF ALL TIME

"What I am going to say will surely cause astonishment and outrage in those who gullibly pray, but Jesus wasn't holy contrary to what priests and pastors say: He was made of flesh and bone and bound to die just like any other guy, or rather, not so ordinary like that, for he was fucking sly like no other under the sky – well, in fact, he was a bit different cos he was a mixed-race Roman Jew and had conspicuous European facial features and height. You know, the Roman soldiers' average height was 5'7" while the Jews' average height was 5'5' – a slight but considerable difference. You see, his height and European facial features were obviously inherited from his father, the Roman soldier Tiberius Julius Abdes Pantera.

So, he was taller than most other Jews of that time and had suntanned white skin; his eyes and hair were dark brown – you see, I think it's kind of interesting to note that he tried to keep both hair and beard trimmed when he was in town.

Just for the record, he learned magic, hypnotism and the science of healing in Egypt, his birthplace – but he was a Jew, or rather, a mixed-race Roman Jew – he had just been born there. Later, he spent some time in India in order to gain more knowledge about the art of magic, hypnotism and healing. In Greece he studied philosophy and sophistic rhetoric to master the art of preaching and influence people in order to reach his goals. Then, after spending about two years abroad, he came back to Egypt and took his mother along back to Palestine.

You see, he was a wise guy who developed a magical and medicinal knowledge superior to the ones of his Egyptian and Indian masters. The same can be said about the sophistic philosophical knowledge he acquired in Greece.

Holy shit, that guy was really the greatest magician of all time! His artful ingenious tricks together with the unbelievable healings he performed were seen as miracles by the gullible ignorant brutish people of his time.

Well, after getting back to the region of Gennesaret, he proclaimed himself the son of God – and proved his claim by duping people with his peerless magic tricks and hypnotic ability, plus his unbelievable healings, which helped him gain more credibility and attract more people to his healing sessions so that he could get enough money to make an easy living.

You see, in order to reach his goals, thru magic tricks and hypnotism, he managed to convince five gullible fishermen that he really was the son of God and had divine powers – I was one of those five suckers. *(laughs)* Then, he first made us his disciples, that is, students, and after teaching us lots of things, mainly the art of persuasion, he named us as his apostles, or rather, in fact he appointed us as sorta like his marketers *(laughs)* – besides, we served also as kinda like his bodyguards. And so, off some of us went ahead of him from city to city to advertise his alleged divine healing powers. You see, I know all these things about him cos he himself told me the whole shebang after we died.

Anyway, in spite of ev'rything, he was altruistic and kind like no other man, though he was a bit of a hothead sometimes – speaking of which, once, he took my sword and furiously cut down a fig tree to the ground just cos he wanted some figs, though there wasn't any, for it wasn't the right season.

You see, I feel it's important to highlight that in the chapter 21:18-22 of the Bible – which was wrongly attributed to a certain Mathew, they wrote that the fig tree withered 'cause Jesus cursed it, but, paraphrasing him: truly I say to you it's not true *(laughs)*. They also wrote that Peter, one of his supposed 12 disciples, called him "Rabbi" and then showed him the withered fig tree; yet, it ain't true either, for "rabbi" is a religious jargon used to name a spiritual leader or religious teacher in Judaism, but Jesus hated all that boring stuff of spirituality and religious teaching – we all knew it damn well and so we would never call him like that.

In fact, in spite of wanting, he knew he couldn't free his people from the Roman dominion, cos he knew it was something beyond his capability. So, he just kinda intended to ease the oppression to which they were subjected through some sort of general strike. He always said that only a fool would start a rebellion and try to overthrow the Romans, 'cause besides resulting in bloodshed and death it would be useless, for the Romans were far more powerful than a bunch of ill-armed Jews that anyone could hypothetically gather. However, the betrayal of Judas, or rather Jed[1], thwarted his plan.

Just for the record, in the Bible they say that Pilate asked the crowd whether they wanted to free Barabbas or Jesus, but it is absolutely untrue,

for the Romans were the rulers of the Middle East territories back then and, so they took all the decisions regarding the administration of them, including, of course, the imposition of law.

Therefore, it's obvious that Pilate wouldn't waste his time asking people which of them should be crucified: whether Jesus, a pacific petty miracle maker, who had been arrested on the basis of an ungrounded accusation or Barabbas, a hardened dangerous robber and murderer. Besides, if he did so, that would show lack of authority and incompetence to rule that region annexed by the Roman Empire. Thus, it's easy to conclude that this whole shebang is just a figment of the imagination of the Greek writers who wrote the New Testament. So, it can easily be concluded that they sent both of them to be crucified, for they would never release such a dangerous criminal like Barabbas.

Furthermore, most of the poor loved Jesus and would never ask for his death, for he healed their sick ones in return for any sum of money or food and many times for free. Besides amazing them with his artful magic tricks, which they thought to be something divine because they were rude and gullible. You see, to those ignorant superstitious credulous Jews, he was, indeed, the son of God.

On the other hand, most rich people, most nobles, most middle-class citizens and all of those envious jealous spiteful temple priests regarded him as just a drunken troublemaker and charlatan.

By the way, he was not crucified on a conventional cross, but rather tortured upside down on a T-shaped one – after being stripped of his clothes and naughty bits *(laughs)*.

Well, it's noteworthy to point out that we, his apostles, shrewdly, made up this resurrection stuff so that people thought he was indeed the son of God and we could keep on making money off his name. In fact, like all the gullible people of that time, we also believed he was the son of God gifted with divine magic powers. But his death on the cross, luckily, inspired us to act like that.

Actually, what really happened was that, in order to achieve our goal, we stole his body and devised this cock-and-bull angel story to give more credibility to the whole shebang.

However, I think I must also point out that, in opposition to what they say in the Bible, there were no soldiers standing guard at his sepulcher, cos the Roman authorities considered him just another ordinary miracle maker and wouldn't waste time on this. Anyway, our shrewdness was so great that even today, many centuries later, people still believe in this Resurrection stuff..."

[1]This name change is explained by the apostle Seth further on.

*by EPHRAIM, ONE OF JESUS FIVE APOSTLES

A DEADLY COMMERCIAL COMPETITION

"As soon as Jesus was warned of the treason of Judas, or rather Jed*, for not being a sucker real quick he fled, but soon was caught hiding under a bed at the house of Jochebed, one of the many lovers he had. *(laughs)* Then, he even attempted to hypnotize those motherfucking Roman soldiers who were hunting for him ev'rywhere, but it didn't work much to his despair – you see, his desperate attempt did fail cos he was under stress fearing that in jail they might fuck his ass. *(laughs)* So, he was arrested and then after being convicted he was taken to the courtyard of Jerusa temple to be crucified... Btw, Jerusa is short for Jerusalem – in fact, that was how most Jews called that purported holy city. Of course, it was pronounced Yehusha in Hebrew, cos Jerusa is the way its shortened form is pronounced in English.

On arriving there, after tying and nailing him upside down to a T-shaped cross they cut off his naughty bits. Then, before they did it, Jesus looked at the guy crucified beside him and thought: "Cursed be the Romans! They're evil to the bone, but at least I'm not alone." *(laughs)*

Just so you know, in the Roman Empire outlaws were executed on special "Egyptian" crosses – called "Tau Crosses", which looked like the letter "T", and not on stereotyped ones as it's shown in the pics portraying Jesus's crucifixion.

On another note, in fact, the name of the guy who betrayed Jesus wasn't Judas, but rather Jedediah*, nicknamed Jed by us, his mates. He was another fisherman in the Sea of Galilee – which is, actually, a freshwater lake close to the village of Gennesaret, which was located very near the rural area where Jesus' mother was born. Note that the pronunciation of Gennesaret is somewhat similar to Nazareth.

Btw, only his followers called him Jesus Christ – to them "Christ" meant something nearly like "the savior"; people in general called him

Jesus of Gennesaret, not Jesus of Nazareth, and some mean persons called him Yeshu – meaning something almost like "the unworthy cursed trickster", for they were taught to do so by the temple priests. Besides, some others mockingly called him Yeshu ben Pantera (Yeshu son of Pantera), Yeshu ben stada (Yeshu son of the adulteress), cos they knew his real father was the Roman soldier nicknamed Pantera, meaning Panther and Jesus, the outlaw – ah, in addition, his mother affectionately called him **Shushu** – a cute nickname derived from his nameYe**shu**a. Btw, this nickname is similar to the French word "chouchou", meaning "dear/ my dear/ darling /honey". It's pronounced as "shoushou" with the stress on the second syllable. You see, in order to get information about it, search for the article entitled "chouchu / French to English", published on the internet by "Proz.com" on 10/14/2003.

Well, just for the record, Jed didn't betray Jesus for only 30 pieces of silver as it's written in the Bible, for that sum of money was worth just a salary paid to an ordinary worker back then, which was a starvation salary, by the way. You see, he told me later that he was given an amount of money worth lots of times more than the salary Jesus' paid us – but as he was a cousin of mine, besides having done a lot of favors to me, I never told this secret to the other apostles. Well, as Jesus paid us good money, it's obvious that Jed wouldn't betray him for any sum of money inferior to his salary. But the temple priests tempted him by offering much more money than he was paid and he couldn't resist. You see, Jed was a degenerate gambler and owed lots of money to a certain moneylender who was threatening to kill him if he didn't pay his money back. Thus, the temple priests, who were in bed with[1] that moneylender *(laughs)*, found out about it and then managed to entice Jed into putting an end to Jesus' commercial competition for the templegoers and their money, apart from other things they donated. That's why he snitched on Jesus to the Romans. I deem it necessary to point out that Judas, or rather, Jed, wasn't the treasurer of Jesus' miracles and healings company as it's written in the bible – I myself was the treasurer of Jesus' company and I never embezzled any money – nor could I 'cos he, meticulously, checked the cash inflow ev'ry single day.

On another note, the names of Jesus' apostles were made up by the money-grubbing shrewd Roman Catholic Church. Besides, there weren't 12 of us, but only five, for he knew it would be financially counterproductive to pay so many workers like that – that's why we were only five, plus 2 more followers he hired to help us later, but he paid them less than half of what he paid us."

[1]in cahoots with.

*by SETH THE JOKER, ONE OF JESUS' FIVE APOSTLES

WHAT DIFFERENCE DOES IT MAKE?

"Believers get pissed off when some people say I was gay, but whether I was gay or not, if it's true or fake, what difference does it make? This is just as relevant as the color of Little Red Riding Hood's toy shopping cart, for sexuality's unrelated to good or evil in man's heart."
   *by JESUS

HOLY SMOKE

On that Sunday worship service, the stoned drunk preacher, whose name was Stan Hermon Chris, cleared his throat and began his sermon like this: "Then, God, after smoking a joint and drinking wine, said in Genesis 1:29: 'On the face of the whole Earth, I give you every plant bearing seed and every tree bearing fruit in it...' – he didn't exclude weed, Holy Shit!..."

DEAD BEFORE STEPPING OUT

He had no idea he had left. Comfortably numb he didn't even suspect he was coming back. He didn't know where he had gone and whether he was alive or dead, whether awake or sleeping in his bed.

When he opened up the eyes in his head, he heard a voice that said, "Welcome back, my dear. Please, have no fear. Now I'm gonna tell you a little bit about the ones who'd be your relatives in that planet inhabited by the evil human race and you'll be glad to have left that damned place. You see, your paternal grandfather is a serial killer crazy for girls, your maternal grandpa is a drug dealer mad for pearls; your fatherly grandmother spends most of her time in jail, she's a petty thief just released on bail, your motherly grandma died from an overdose of smack near a smokestack; your mother sells her body to buy crack and smoke with your brother Mack, your father is a drunkard named Clark, a poor bastard who sleeps in the park... Anyway, I'm sure it was really better for you not to have come out to see the light and go thru such a terrible plight. You see, son, down there on Earth things are getting worse and worse to the poor: left at the mercy of poverty, disease, hunger and war. Moreover, in that damned place where life is a nightmare ev'ryone is born doomed to die. So, for not having been born there you're such a lucky guy..."

So, what's next? Will Jack remain up there in heaven hiding from fate forever and a day? Or will God send him back to reincarnate as a straight or as a gay? – Well, God might as well act friendly towards Jack and not send him back to be put to the rack and scavenge for his next meal in some third world landfill always feelin' his life is goin' downhill. Anyway, be that as it may, let us pray that they can make a deal so that at least he may be reborn as a seal...

EARTH VS. THE HUMAN VIRUS

So that you can understand what I will say next I must speak about the Gaia theory, which was created by the English scientist James Lovelock. Well, to sum it up, according to his theory Earth is a kind of living organism. So, she also tries to eliminate the pathogens that cause her harm just like us – and who are these pathogens? Obvious answer: human beings. Earth view human beings as pathogens, so, to her, we are something like deadly viruses. Btw, you can find further information about the Gaia theory in the article entitled "Gaia Theory, created by James Lovelock, describes Earth as a...", published on the internet by "Oxbow School".

In order that you get full comprehension of the subject under discussion, I must also explain what is Panspermia. Well, Panspermia is, in short, a theory according to which life on Earth came from outer space aboard meteorites. "This theory was actually first mentioned by the Greek philosopher Anaxagoras – btw, the term "panspermia" was coined by him. By the way, to get more information about the Panspermia Theory, search for the text entitled "Early Life Theories – Panspermia Theory", published on the internet by "ThoughtCo" on 01/30/2018."

So, my friend Sam and I elaborated our own theory stemming from the panspermia. Well, according to our theory, the molecules aboard the meteorites that brought our space forefathers were designed to form only male humanoid creatures, so, obviously, no females were formed after they crashed on Earth. This way, when they grew up, they started having homosexual relationships, for there were no females to copulate with. Yet, they soon realized that the animals around them, besides having sexual intercourse too, procreated – therefore giving continuity to their species. So, they got worried because they realized that as they did not procreate, their species one day would **cease to exist**.

So, they looked around more attentively and saw that there were some animals that resembled them – namely monkeys. Thus, from then on, they captured females of a species of monkey that resembled them most, besides being more docile, and started fornicating with them. So, when the mixed-race female monkeys reached reproductive age, which happened after their first period, the space-sent males set their mothers free and started having sex with them. And, strange as it may seem, in spite of being hybrid creatures they oddly had reproductive capacity – besides being more sexually attractive than their simian genitrixes for sure. By the way, it's noteworthy that, moreover, they left us the stub of a tail as a legacy to somehow kinda keep their memory alive. *(laughs)*

Thus, from then on, they kept copulating with their daughters, granddaughters, great-granddaughters, great-great-granddaughters and so on for several generations. Until one day all their children became identical to them. So, the homo sapiens, or rather, the human virus was born as a result of the crossbreeding between space-sent males and female monkeys. This way, over the centuries, ev'ry space-sent male has integrated himself into the human society and now leads a rather ordinary life like any other man. You can bet your life that at this very moment they are around fornicating as much as they can. *(laughs)*

Well, of course, all these theories mentioned previously may seem absurd, but nothing is absurd when it's compared to the theory of creation, according to which a supernatural being called God created the universe, Earth and life in 6 days – being that in the last of them he created man and woman thru the process of spontaneous generation – a far-fetched theory according to which life comes from inanimate matter. Such an absurd illogical theory was supplanted by the one of biogenesis, according to which ev'ry living being has its origin in another pre-existing living being. This theory was proven by the French scientist Louis Pasteur, so it stopped being a theory and became a scientific fact.

Btw, in order to get further information about the previous theories, search the Web for the article entitled "Explain the theory of biogenesis", published on the internet by "Vedantu" on 09/26/2020.

Over the centuries, Earth's discomfort caused by the human virus increased more and more due to the rampant growth of its harmful crazy deadly population, which brought pollution and deforestation along. Next, we will give you a brief summary of Earth's attacks against the human virus.

One of these attacks became known as the Antonine Plague and happened in the second century. In order to exterminate the human virus, Earth sent an army of smallpox viruses. This attack killed 5 million human viruses – it seems like a lot, but this viral family proliferates rampantly at a frightening rate and had already reached the number of 200 million viruses by then.

Earth got frustrated and furious, but she did not give up. So, she withdrew her army and in the sixth century she sent another army – no longer formed by viruses, but composed by bacteria of the species Yersinia Pestis. This strike became known as the Justinian Plague. It killed just 30 million human viruses, a rather insignificant number, for their viral population had already reached the staggering number of 300 million pathogens! Because their proliferation is continuous and progressive. So, once again, Earth's attack failed. Feeling even more frustrated and furious than before, she withdrew her army once more – but continued to train her legions of viruses and bacteria...

In 1343, with a better trained army formed by mutants of our old acquaintance Yersinia Pestis, Earth attacked again. That attack became known as the Black Death, for the bacteria caused black spots on the skin of the human-viruses affected by the them. This attack was more efficient and killed 75 million human viruses, but sadly their destructive dangerous deadly viral population had already reached the mind-blowing number of 370 million pathogens – so, it was just another unsuccessful attack and the human virus population kept on proliferating unstoppably to Earth's frustration... Thus, in 1800 it had already reached the astonishing number of 1 billion pathogens!

Poor Earth, she desperately kept on drinking rivers of natural remedies, but unfortunately, they couldn't overcome her illness. Then, she sent hurricanes, tsunamis, earthquakes and storms just to vent the fury caused by her frustration, for they killed few human viruses and, sadly, weren't able to exterminate them once and for all. But one thing's for sure, she will never give up on her uncompromising determination of exterminating the deadly harmful human virus…

In 1918 Earth attacked once more with an army of swine flu viruses backed by mercenary bacteria. This strike became known as "the Spanish Flu" and killed 50 million human viruses, but their damn population had already reached the mind-blowing number of about 1.9 billion viruses; so it was just another failed attempt…

In 2003 she made another assault – this one became known as SARS-COV1 and was carried out by an army of viruses of the corona species supported by mercenary bacteria too – it killed only less than 1000 human viruses…

In 2012, a new strike – it became known as MERS-COV and was executed by that same army of corona virus supported by mercenary bacteria too – yet, much to Earth's frustration, it killed even fewer human viruses than the previous attack. It's important to point out that starting from 1918 onward, all Earth's raids were made by armies of viruses backed by mercenary bacteria…

In 2019, she attacked again – this attack became known as SARS-COV 2. Once again, it was carried out by an army of Corona viruses backed by mercenary bacteria as usual, but way more aggressive than their previous relatives. This time it soon spread across the world and became a global pandemic. It has killed over 15 million human viruses so far and keeps on killing them – though rather moderately now, much to Earth's sorrow.

Btw, in order to get detailed information about the plagues mentioned in this text, search for the article entitled "The worst epidemics and pandemics in history", published on the internet by "Live

Science" on 01/31/23. Besides, you can also find information about such topic on umpteen other sites on the Web.

Well, much to Earth's delight and to ev'ryone's dismay, the corona virus has come to stay. You see, the corona virus is a mutant warrior part of a better prepared army sent by Mother Earth – it's an anomalous pathogen, different from other previous known viruses and mutates frighteningly faster than all of them – it mutates 2 times faster than the H1N1 virus, which caused the Spanish Flu, for example – though it is far less deadly than that microbe.

And to top it all off, it has already associated with other pathogens existing in the necroslurry – a viscous liquid resulting from the decomposition of decaying corpses, which contaminates both soil and groundwater – and what makes it even worse is that such contamination has been occurring for thousands of years...

You know, Corona virus' initial mission was to exterminate the human virus once and for all, but something went wrong with its replication process and its variants instead of becoming more aggressive and deadlier became milder and less lethal, just as it happened in the Spanish Flu Pandemic – after about the same time span. So, in fact, the human virus was saved by that failure in the corona virus replication process and not by the vaccines.

Be that as it may, you're left with no other option than to expect that the worse may happen at any moment, when any other more powerful deadlier pathogen pops out of the blue and start killing the evil human virus mercilessly and unstoppably till their total extermination. Not to mention the fact that the Corona virus keeps killing thousands of human viruses daily.

So, you better start praying, though it's useless, but at least it will give you some consolation derived from wishful thinking. Nevertheless, one thing's for sure: Earth will give no respite to the human virus till she exterminates it once and for all.

EVIL IS COLOR-BLIND

"Some people say Jesus was black – but it's easy to detect a certain weird kind of implicit reverse color discrimination connotation in what they say. But no matter what color he was anyway or even if he was straight or gay. What really matters is that he was the most kind-hearted guy that ever walked under the sky – besides being also fucking sly. *(laughs)* You see, good and evil ain't color-related – furthermore, no matter the color of your skin after your dying day, for it'll be devoured by worms or by flames the same way – not the ones of hell, but those of some crematory whether it's near or far away, no matter if you're straight or gay.

Anyway, one thing you must always keep in mind: Evil is color blind."

*by ZACH, ONE OF JESUS' FIVE APOSTLES

SHAME ON YOU, GOD!

"According to the Bible, God put a baby in Mary's belly on the sly, though they say it wasn't so – Shame on him for doin' that even knowing she was married to old Joe.

Driven by lust he copulated with Joe's pretty young wife leading her to cheat on him and throw dust in her old husband's eyes. So, to hide his lustful deed he duped his stupid minions into believing the biggest of all lies." *(laughs)*

*by SETH THE JOKER, ONE OF JESUS' FIVE APOSTLES

HERE AND IN THE BEYOND TOO

"The poor are tough stubborn creatures who never surrender to dismay: they live by hope and faith and grow poorer day by day. They're gullible, usually ugly and make lots of children who usually go astray.

There is, yet, the certainty that they will rest someday: when death comes and takes them away. But only if there's nothing in the beyond, cos if there's something there as well, they'll escape inferno to face hell; cos it doesn't matter if a poor man's name is Nate, Homer Arnold Carlson, Brother Juan or whatever: his fate is to suffer in this world and also in the other one forever.

Heaven, such a noble and cozy place where the rich go and live damn well ain't no territory for the scabby poor. What's left for them is just suffering first in purgatory and then in hell forever more." *(laughs)*

*by SETH THE JOKER, ONE OF JESUS' FIVE APOSTLES

BEFORE GOING TO HELL

"Being poor is a fucking scary humiliating thing. Being poor is something ev'ry poor hates being.

    The dream of ev'ry poor here, there and ev'rywhere is to become a millionaire so that he can humiliate and oppress his equals as well before he dies and God sends him to hell. Just the same way he is now humiliated and oppressed by the motherfucking rich, cos like them he's also a cocksucking son of a bitch."

*by Seth the joker, one of Jesus' five apostles.

MORBID CRUELTY

Life is a disgusting, scary and gory fucking hairy horror story, where humans are the creepiest of all predators, besides making lots of money off waging wars. We're bloodthirsty evil greedy creatures who keep turning Earth into a giant landfill, but ironically, we call ourselves earthlings, meaning something nearly like "children of the Earth". I mean, if Earth was our mother we shouldn't be killing her, but since we're committing such a brutal crime driven by our self-destructive lethal instincts, we're in fact a crazy bunch of mean matricidal-suicidal varmints.

I mean, we're creeps always ready to rob, steal and kill our own fellow human beings. The fact is, we're so mean and ostentatious to the point of not taking pleasure in just having things for our own well-being galore. You see, our greatest pleasure comes from oppressing and debasing the weaker and the poor.

The naked truth is that 101% out of 100% of all rich people keep in their dirty greedy minds the sadistic pleasure of having far more money than they need, not to bring them wealth and happiness, but to debase and trample on those belonging to the lower class.

But don't fool yourself into thinking the poor are just humble kind-hearted beings cruelly oppressed and humiliated by the rich – evil money-grubbing fuckers who keep them under their sway, for in fact the poor are nothing like that in any way. I mean, if, hypothetically, they became rich too they sure would oppress and demean the ones of their former social class – on that you can bet your sweet ass...

STUCK IN THE SHIT

If the rich shared their money with the poor, they would also become poor for sure. I mean, if such a thing happened, it would not put an end to poverty rise, but the rich would also get stuck in the shit likewise.

Well, the fact is, the rich are not the ones to blame for poverty – politicians are guilty of this shit, for the tax money is used for theirs an' not for people's benefit. That's why you should not be blind and always keep in mind: "Ask not what you can do for your country, for there's nothing you can do, ask instead what your country can do for you".

*A certain politician once said: "Ask not what your country can do for you, ask what you can do for your country." But he who is wise and endowed with critical thinking knows it's actually the other way around.

GOD AND THE COW (cont.)

"In India they venerate the cow as a sacred animal and westerners think it's funny and nonsensical, but it ain't nothing like that – cos at least cows are something that you can see and touch, besides being tame and useful. So, considering a cow as a sacred animal is more logical, rational and wiser than worshipping a god that belongs to Jewish mythology.

Well, anyway, the years rolled by one way or another, indifferent to ev'ryone and their mother, and in 325 AD, about 292 years after the bizarre crucifixion of his self-proclaimed son – a guy imbued with the strange improbable mix of capitalism and altruism, such mythology was officially coopted by the Romans in the first council of Nicaea, convened by the Roman emperor Constantine I – occasion in which key articles of faith were manipulated, formalized and officialized. Then, Yahweh, God's Jewish name, was changed into "**Deus**", the Latin word for God – they renamed him after the name of the supreme Greek god "**Z**eus" – they just replaced "**Z**" by "**D**". To get more information about the facts mentioned previously in this paragraph, search the Web for the text entitled "A Concise History of the Roman Catholic Church" by Mary Fairchild, published by "Learn Religions" on 06/25/2019.

Later, the New Testament, which had been translated from Geek into Latin, was translated into English and the name "**Deus**" became "**God**", a moniker derived from the word "**dog**" – you see, the derivation process consisted in just writing it backwards." *(laughs)*.

*by SETH THE JOKER, ONE OF JESUS FIVE APOSTLES

HE WILL NEVER COME BACK (cont.)

"Christians, whether they're straight or gay white or black, zealously say Jesus will come back. Yet, they're dead-wrong, because he is a wise guy – now even wiser than he musta been, and will never return to this pigsty we live in. Besides, he is too old – he is already 2024 or maybe more – so, he's afraid that covid-19 may kill him, since he has severe comorbidities due to old age and ain't willing to take no chances at this stage. *(laughs)*

Moreover, he ain't willing to run the risk of, once more, wearing another fucking crown of thorns like before. Well, he told me he'll never more step on Earth like he did long ago, just so you know, cos he is sure that if he returns they'll put on his head a crown that will deliver continuous electrical shocks to his bollocks." *(laughs)*

*by SETH THE JOKER, ONE OF JESUS' FIVE APOSTLES

FROM BEYOND THE GRAVE

(COMMENTS FROM ANONYMOUS SPIRITS)

AT LEAST I DIED WITH MY EAR ON

"The night that good-for-nothing motherfucking scumbag came to my house he brought two girls along – I remember we smoked weed together some time ago, but I can't remember their names… Well, after entering my house, he told me he wanted his money back, cos I had sold him bad drugs and the guys he had resold the drug to were after him. *(laughs)* So, he wanted his money back to return it to them in order to calm things down. But I said I didn't have the money anymore and he didn't believe me for sure. After that, he gave the gun to one of the girls and told her to shoot me if I made any suspicious move. Next, he started looking for the money throughout the room… I realized the girl wouldn't shoot, for she looked too nervous, so I lunged at her and took the gun… then, she started screaming in panic that I had taken the gun… next, he pounced on me and we began to fight… during the fight the gun fell from my hand and slipped under an armchair, but, hell, that good-for-nothing cocksucker managed to get a knife he kept inside his boot and slashed my face close to my ear; then, he stuck that fucking knife straight into my heart killing me… well, after all, it wasn't so bad like that, for at least I died with my ear on. *(laughs)* So, after a while, he and the girls went away taking along only some weed they found stashed somewhere – an amount enough to roll just some four or five joints at most…" *(laughs)*

*by X

BLOODY WEED

"...so, we went away and left him there sprawled on the floor, blood leaking out of his wound... We both were horrified and google-eyed because we didn't ever think that thing could happen before our eyes. Well, our friend said he didn't mean to kill him and that it was all just an accident. In fact, we didn't know anything about what was going on between them... we went along just to visit him, hang out together and smoke some weed, for we kinda liked that good-for-nothing motherfucking petty drug dealer... Anyway, at least, we got a little weed and rolled us some joints..." *(laughs)*

*by Y

JOHN DOE

"Noah's Ark tale is a far-fetched story fabricated by the fertile imagination of some ancient stoned Jewish writer. Only people who are damn gullible believe that all those wild beasts would tamely enter that fucking ark, brother, and live together peacefully without devouring or killing each other. Besides, the amount of food necessary to feed all those beasts, always at war, would be so large that it would be impossible to store – for example, where would they store the meat for the alligator if there was no refrigerator?..."

JANE DOE

"It's laughable how believers view as an unquestionable truth what is written in this so-called Holy Writ, despite being so easy to see most of its content is just bullshit."

HIS HOLINESS THINGAMASHIT

"Jesus Christ did not die for anyone; this is just a foolish belief based on blind faith and credulity of course. Hell, he died for not being able to resist torture like no other would even if he was a horse."

MR. SO-AND-SO

"Believers regard as true the far-fetched nonsensical story stating that at the communion ceremony Jesus becomes wine and bread, but this is just bullshit that was instilled into their head."

MISS WHATSERNAME

"Believers have no doubt that Jesus did walk on the water. Yet, it's written that he walked on the water only after he sent the crowd away, so only his apostles were eyewitnesses to that supposed fact. Duh, it's evident that this far-fetched story was made up by him and spread around by his apostles, you see."

NOBODY

"It's said that Jesus spoke the following words to the crowd: 'Blessed are the poor, for theirs is the kingdom of heaven forevermore.' Well, he might well have said: 'Blessed are the rich, for the kingdom of heaven belongs to them the whole eternity thru. They enjoy it now and in the afterlife too.' You see, who can guarantee the words they say he spoke are true and not those I just said to you?"

MRS. THINGUMMY

"The poor's plight will change for the better of course, but only when the rider carries the horse. In fact, things are bad only for them, but not for the rich – fuckers who worship money as their God and live a life of pleasure and luxury, while the poor waste their time asking God for help foolishly, unable to see God's just what you call fortuity. Besides being fruit of credulity and gullibility."

LORD THINGAMAFUCK

"If the so-called law of cause and effect, which supposedly punishes people for the evil deeds they do along their lives, really exists, it affects only the poor: gullible suckers that do not have a pot in which to piss, not the rich, lucky fuckers who use their money to buy lots of bliss."

SOMEONE OR OTHER

"The story of Jesus's resurrection isn't based on reality, but rather on folklore and mythology, though Christians believe in this stuff blindly. But what happened, in fact, was that his apostles stole his body so that people thought he resurrected for being a holy man, cos such a story would make it possible for them to keep on making an easy living like he did before. I mean, they just followed his example.

You see, they shrewdly realized that if they did so, they could go on making money off his name, for at that point Jesus had already achieved widespread fame. In addition, contrary to what is said in the Bible, there were no soldiers standing guard outside his sepulcher, for the Romans regarded him as just another petty miracle maker like so many others that wandered throughout that region back then. And to top it all off, they cannily made up that story of this angel that popped out of the blue and made the supposed guards faint. They did so to boost their lie, for somehow, they already knew that a lie told often enough becomes the truth."

MR. WHOEVER

"There are about 2.5 billion Christians in the world, so there are also the same number of Gods: one for every Christian in reality; for God's singular, though at the same time he's a plural entity, besides being also a personal deity.

You see, whenever someone starts following Christianity, his individual God is born as well. When he dies, his personal God also dies and both go to hell." *(laughs)*

SOME POEMS

NOW IS THE ONLY THING REAL

No matter who'll eat the fruit of the tree you may grow
Seeds of love always try hard to sow
Ev'rywhere that you go.
You won't find only love, but also hate along the road
But what matters is the love in your heart you hold.
Instead of bullets may ev'ry gun shoot flowers and fun
Instead of hate let there only be love for ev'ryone
May all people share riches before life's done.
Now is the only thing real as once a man said
Cos when later comes you may well be dead
So, outta your heart make an airfield
Oh, where only solidarity lands
And for evil deeds try hard to make amends.
Let there not be any more wars
And no room too for greed, fear and hunger
May man drop chocolate bars
And not shells from the bomber.

NEVER GIVE UP THE FIGHT

As you can still fight, fight with all your might,
Never give up the fight.
All thru the night you'll be alright; in the end you'll find the light.
Cheer up, cut the ties linking to inner fears
An' let fun come to wash away all your tears.
Thru the maze of this life each an' ev'ry poor
Go thru hell ev'ry day
For to evil-hearted people they easily fall prey...
Anyway, living and dying are parts of the same cyclic game
In which the score is always the same...
To the poor, life is damn bed, they rest only when they're dead,
To them the world's so wrong, they're just pariahs
In the countries to which they belong...
In man's cruel heart, ole greed breeds war
Destroy lives and brings lots of gore.
Anyway, let's hope peace come to lead the way toward a new day...
The fact is whether you play well or not the score is always the same
Ev'ry move is in vain
Cos in the end you will lose the game...

OUTTA CONTROL

Come on, babe, come on, let's do something good:
I'll be your eater, you'll be my food.
I got a hungry body to feed, you got what I want
I got what you need.
I just wanna have fun,
Come on, let's copulate till the night's done.
Girl, forget all of your sorrow, do not think of tomorrow
Just love me with all your might and ev'ything will be alright.
Tonight I'm the devil outta control,
But I want your body and not your soul
There's only us here, we're all alone
So, let's have fun all night long.
Tonight thru pleasure's maze I'll be your guide
Babe, spread your wings and let me come inside
Come to get my worries on the run
Come on, let's fornicate wild and strong
Uncaring about what is right or wrong
Playing damn glad like a pope and a nun
Upon the bed doing dope and having fun...

GOD AIN'T ON YOUR SIDE

In fear you wonder why a cloudy dark sky
Don't let the sun shine though it's high summertime...
Then you suddenly hear booms an' shots ev'rywhere
An' in the blink of an eye it all become nightmare.
Whoa, it's always too late When the devil draft you to dwell forever in hell...
Oh, it's like quick sand, useless to cry,
At least, my friend, alone you won't die.
So, fast you wanna run an' find a place to hide,
But you can find none,
Cos God ain't on your side...
So, no use calling him, nothing he can do
Because the game is over for you...
Oh, it's as if you were drowning, you sink like a stone,
But at least, my friend, you won't die alone.
No way to get out of this deadly game,
Even God is trying to do the same.
So, no use calling him, for nothing he can do
Because he is running for shelter too...

THE SAME OLD SHIT ALL OVER AGAIN

Xmas is the time o' jingle bells, joy an' wine,
Love is in the air in this special date
An' you help the poor fulfill their needs,
But along the year in your heart there's only hate
An' you always do bad deeds.
Wish you a fuckin' merry Xmas an' a damn good new year
The old will be over an' the new one is near
It'll bring the same troubles that afflict ev'ryone
Besides bringin' new ones to spoil all the fun.
They are all out to get both you an' me,
So, you better stop your hypocrisy.
Xmas is the time to wait for Santa Claus
An' his red bag full o' gifts of ev'ry kind,
However, meanwhile, to kill your neighbor
Is the thought you keep in mind...

DISCLAIMER

This is a work of fiction. Any references to historical events, real people or real places are used fictitiously. The names of all the characters in this book are figments of the authors' imagination.